HOW THE OCELOTS GOT THEIR SPOTS

Lyle Stuart, Inc.
120 Enterprise Avenue
Secaucus, N. J. 07094

HOW THE OCELOTS GOT THEIR SPOTS

by Ireene Wicker

illustrated by Catherine Perrot

First edition
Copyright © 1976 by Ireene Wicker and Catherine Perrot
All rights reserved
Published by Lyle Stuart, Inc.
120 Enterprise Ave., Secaucus, N.J. 07094
In Canada: George J. McLeod Limited
73 Bathurst St., Toronto, Ont.
Manufactured in the United States of America

Designed by David H. Robbins

Library of Congress Cataloging in Publication Data

Perrot, Catherine.
  How the ocelots got their spots.

  SUMMARY: Relates how the ocelots got their spots
with the help of the Butterfly Man and his pots of
colors.
  [1. Ocelots—Fiction. 2. Colors—Fiction]
I. Wicker, Ireene. II. Title.
PZ7.P4344Ho   [E]   75-43887
ISBN 0-8184-0231-8

HOW THE OCELOTS GOT THEIR SPOTS

Once upon a time, before ocelots and wild cats had any spots, there were two beautiful ocelots, Babou and his mate, Bouba.

One day Babou and Bouba were lying comfortably on a large branch of the tallest tree in the biggest forest of the biggest jungle in South America. It was morning, and it was a sunny day, and they were very happy, for they were kind and good and they enjoyed doing things together.

Bouba looked at her mate and whispered into his ear, "What shall we do today, Babou? Shall we search for food? Shall we visit our parents and brothers and sisters? Or should we just stay here and run and play?"

Babou replied, "Well Bouba, let us look at it this way. There is plenty of food in our cave, and we visited our parents and brothers and sisters yesterday. Why don't we enjoy this lovely day all by ourselves?"

Bouba said, "What a truly marvelous idea!"

Once that was settled, they relaxed under the warm rays of the sun. They were very quiet, and Babou had almost fallen asleep when Bouba suddenly cried, "Babou! Look there! Look at that strange little man!"

Babou looked in the direction that Bouba pointed her paw. "How interesting," he said. "We have seen human being men before, but this gentleman has two mustaches that go up into the air like two antennas!"

"How strange," said Bouba.

"How peculiar," said Babou.

"See how he sits with that cape around his shoulders. It makes him look like a giant butterfly. What ever do you think he is doing?" asked Bouba.

"I don't know," said Babou. "Let us sit here quietly and observe him."

"I believe he should be called the Butterfly Man," remarked Bouba.

"What a very good idea!" said Babou.

The two ocelots sat very still. They watched the strange little man who was doing such strange things. He held a thin stick in his hand and seemed to be using it to hit a piece of canvas that he had standing before him.

After awhile the sun went down, and it began to get cloudy.

"Do not dally," Bouba said aloud to herself, "for if you dally, Babou and I cannot go over to see what you have done!"

Almost as if he heard her, the little man suddenly stood up, put the stick in his pocket, and drew his cape closely about himself. Then he picked up the canvas with both hands and walked away.

"Babou! Let's go down to see if we can learn what he was doing!"

"All right, Bouba. Let's do!"

Gracefully jumping from one branch to the other, Babou and Bouba made their way down to the ground. When they came to where the strange little Butterfly Man had been, they saw that he had left a wooden box. It had a handle which Babou promptly poked at with his paws. Soon he had it open.

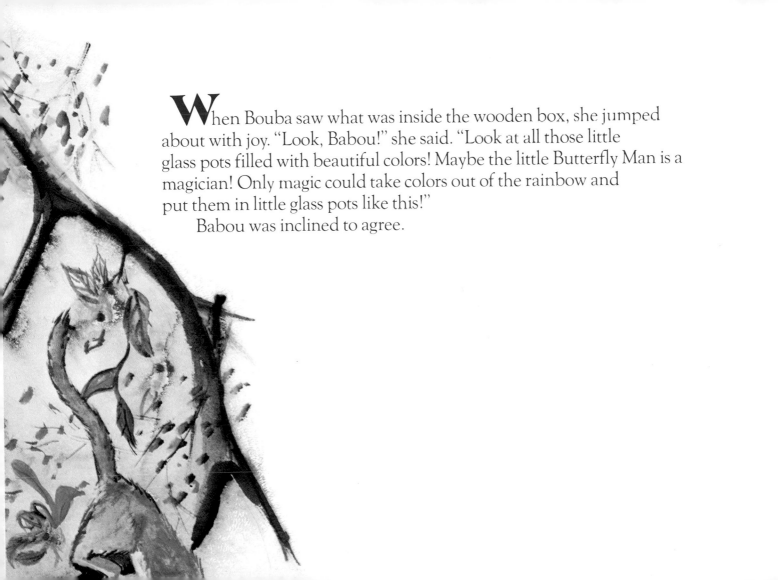

When Bouba saw what was inside the wooden box, she jumped about with joy. "Look, Babou!" she said. "Look at all those little glass pots filled with beautiful colors! Maybe the little Butterfly Man is a magician! Only magic could take colors out of the rainbow and put them in little glass pots like this!"

Babou was inclined to agree.

Then Bouba had another idea. "Babou! Let's use the colors to make everything beautiful!"

"That's a marvelous idea, Bouba! Let's do! The yellow will make the grass look like a cornfield!"

"Yes! And the red and the blue and the white will make the bushes and the plants and even the weeds look like flowers!"

They put the colors on everything, having a lot of fun doing it. Suddenly Babou noticed that all the bright colors of the rainbow had been used up. Only the brown and black pots of color were left. He clapped his hands happily.

"Bouba! I have an idea!"

"Oh, tell me! Tell me!" said Bouba.

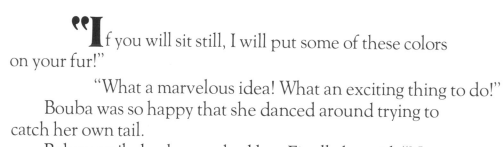

"**I**f you will sit still, I will put some of these colors on your fur!"

"What a marvelous idea! What an exciting thing to do!"
Bouba was so happy that she danced around trying to catch her own tail.

Babou smiled as he watched her. Finally he said, "Now you must sit still and be quiet." Then he dipped one paw into the pot of brown and the other into the pot of black. He rubbed his paws on Bouba's back.

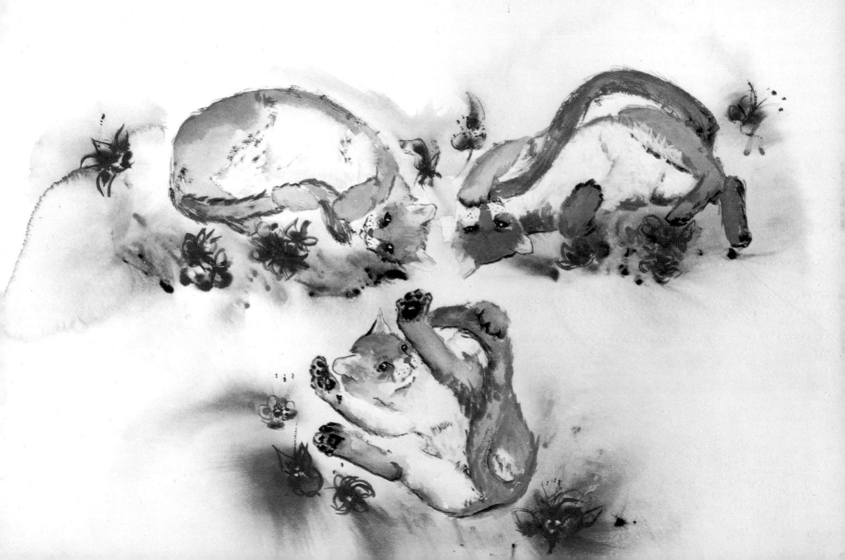

"**W**hat are you doing, Babou?" she asked.

"I am painting a snake around your neck and down your back."

"A snake?"

"Yes, because a snake is our worst enemy, except for the eagle," he explained. "We can see the eagle because he comes from the sky, so we can hide. If an eagle should try to catch us by surprise, we can defend ourselves with our strong paws. But snakes are tricky. They slink around on the ground so that we don't always see them. Now you have lines and spots on your back muscles. When you move, the lines and spots will move."

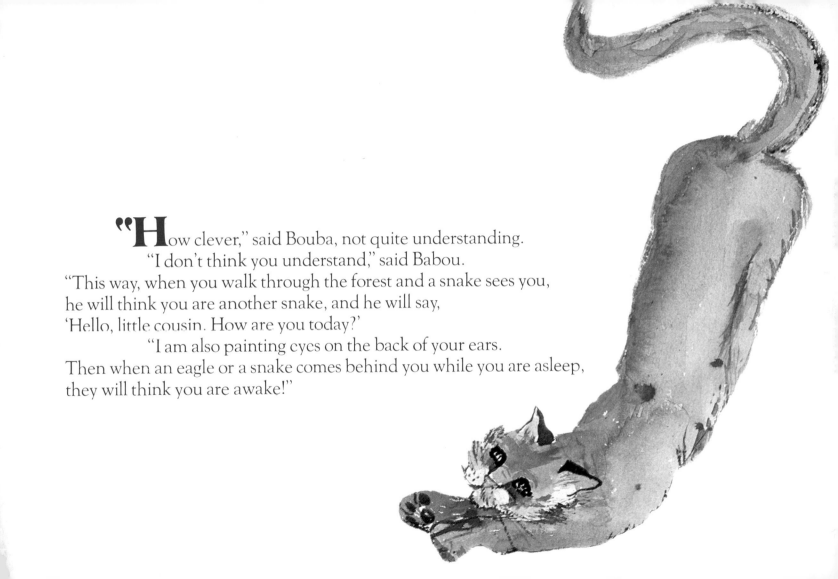

"**H**ow clever," said Bouba, not quite understanding.
        "I don't think you understand," said Babou.
"This way, when you walk through the forest and a snake sees you,
he will think you are another snake, and he will say,
'Hello, little cousin. How are you today?'
        "I am also painting eyes on the back of your ears.
Then when an eagle or a snake comes behind you while you are asleep,
they will think you are awake!"

"How marvelous!" said Bouba. "How truly marvelous!"
Babou was secretly pleased that Bouba thought him clever.
This caused him to have another idea. "Now I shall draw on your
eyelashes. If you are asleep and an enemy comes in front of you, he will
also think you are awake and run away!"

"Oh, Babou! You are the very smartest ocelot in this
entire jungle. What makes you think of such marvelous
things to do?"

"My love for you, Bouba," said Babou. "I love you and I
want to protect you."

"How very nice. What will you do next, Babou?"

"Now I will make up your beautiful eyes so they look
like those of a lovely Oriental lady. On your sides I will make a tortoise
shell and on your white tummy, lovely black spots."

Babou did just what he said he would do. Then he stepped back
to look at Bouba.

"How do I look?" asked Bouba.

"You are lovely to look at," said Babou. "In addition to being beautiful, you are protected too."

Bouba jumped up and down happily. Then she dipped her tail into the color pots and ran to Babou. "Now, dear Babou, I shall do for you what you have done for me!"

And she did. First she painted the lines of the snake on Babou's back.
Then she did the spots and the tortoise shell. Since Babou
had done it first, it was easy for Bouba to copy what he had done.

They had been playing for so long that now evening had come. The moon shone down on them.

"Babou, let's go to the lake where we get our drinking water. We can look at ourselves in the moonlight that shines on the water."

Without waiting for an answer, she was off and running. Babou bounded after her.

Bouba looked at herself in the reflection in the lake, and she was delighted. She reached over and kissed Babou.

"I am so pleased, dear Babou," she said. "This is the most beautiful coat I have ever worn!"

Babou smiled and patted her paw. He too was pleased.

On the way back to their tree, they met a snake.
Before they could be afraid, the snake greeted them in friendly
forest language.

"Hello little cousins! How attractive you look today!"
Babou and Bouba thanked the snake and walked away. When they
were out of the snake's sight, they laughed happily.

"It worked! It worked! The snake was fooled!"
they both said.

That night, Babou and Bouba had one of their nicest sleeps.
It was because they had so much fun with the colors and
because now they felt so safe from snakes and eagles.

The next morning when they awoke, they heard a loud noise in the distance. When they looked, they saw that the strange little man, with his two mustaches and his big, butterfly cape, had returned. He saw that all his beautiful colors had been spilled on the grass, the bushes, and the weeds. He looked unhappy.

"Bouba, dear," said Babou, "we must go and tell the Butterfly Man how sorry we are that we took his colors."

"Yes, Bouba," said Babou. "We must indeed."

Down the tree they went. They went to the Butterfly Man. He was very surprised to see them. His eyes became larger, and his mustaches wiggled.

After Babou and Bouba had apologized, the Butterfly Man threw his hands in the air and shouted happily, "How fantastic! It is a masterpiece! This is no act of tiddly-winks! It is a work of wonder!"

"Then you are not angry because we used your colors?" said Bouba?

"Angry? No no no! I am happy that you used my colors. From this day on we shall always be friends!"

And so they were.

The Butterfly Man painted ocelots many times after that. Then, some time later, Bouba became the mother of twin babies. And guess what! Those baby ocelots had exactly the same spots as their mother and father!

Even today, all ocelots have those same beautiful spots. Everyone admires their beautiful coats because they are protective as well as beautiful.

The ocelots lived happily ever after. And now you too know the legend of how the ocelots got their spots.